Editor's Note

Here are three tales of enchantment,
	Beauty and the Beast,
	The Frog Prince,
	and The Six Swans.
In each story one or more persons have been transformed
into animals. Only love, faithfulness to a promise, and
devotion can break the spells.

Beauty and the Beast was adapted from the classic
story by Madame Leprince de Beaumont. It was first
published in English in Madame de Beaumont's "The
Young Misses Magazine" in 1761. Though The Frog
Prince is a very old folk story, it was written down in
complete form for the first time by Jacob and Wilhelm
Grimm, who also wrote The Six Swans. Both tales were
published in German in the early 1800s. The versions that
appear in this book were adapted from early English
translations.

BEAUTY AND THE BEAST

and Other Tales of Enchantment

Illustrated by Jane Chambless-Rigie

A GOLDEN BOOK • NEW YORK

Western Publishing Company, Inc., Racine, Wisconsin 53404

Beauty and the Beast

THERE WAS once a rich merchant who had three daughters. They were all very pretty, especially the youngest. She was so lovely, she was called Beauty.

Beauty was as good as she was beautiful, but her sisters thought they were better than anyone else. They made fun of Beauty because she spent most of her time at home reading good books.

Then, quite suddenly, the merchant lost his fortune. All he had left was a small country house. Sadly, he told his children they must move there.

When the family arrived at the country house, the merchant set about farming. Beauty rose at four every morning to do the chores and cook the meals. After she was finished with her work, Beauty read or played music. Her two sisters got up at ten and did nothing but complain all day. "What a stupid creature Beauty is to be contented with such a dull life!" said one to the other.

The good merchant did not agree. He knew very well that Beauty outshone her sisters, in her mind as well as her person.

The family had lived in the country about a year when the merchant received a letter. It said one of the ships he had given up for lost had arrived safely in port with a rich cargo. As he made ready to leave, his two oldest daughters begged him to bring them new gowns, hats, and all kinds of trinkets when he returned.

"And what will you have, Beauty?" asked the merchant.

"Since you have asked me," answered Beauty, "bring me a rose, for none grow here."

    The good man went on his journey, but when he arrived, he found his former partner had already claimed the cargo. After a great deal of trouble, the merchant turned homeward as poor as when he had left.

    When he had thirty miles to go, he got lost in a great forest. The poor merchant feared he would die of cold and hunger if the wolves did not eat him first. Then he saw a light through the trees. He struggled toward it and came to a palace lit from top to bottom.

The merchant was surprised to see no one around, but his horse, seeing a large stable open, went in and began to eat. The merchant left it there and walked to the palace.

He entered a large hall and found a blazing fire on the hearth and a table heaped with food and one place set. He sat down by the fire to dry himself.

"I hope," he said, "the master of the house will not mind. I suppose he or one of his servants will come soon."

The merchant waited a long time, but at last he was so hungry, he sat down at the table and ate until he could eat no more.

Afterward he left the hall and walked through several magnificent rooms until he came to one that had a comfortable looking bed in it. As he was very tired, the merchant shut the door and went to sleep.

When he awoke, he was astonished to see a new suit of clothes in place of his own, which were spoiled. "This place must belong to a fairy," he said, "who has seen and pitied my distress."

He looked through a window and saw a garden filled with beautiful flowers. The merchant returned to the great hall, where he found some hot chocolate. "Thank you, good Fairy," he said aloud. "I am grateful for all your favors."

The good man drank his chocolate and went to get his horse. Passing through an arbor of roses, he remembered Beauty's request and picked a branch with several flowers. Immediately, he heard a terrible roar and saw a frightful Beast coming towards him.

"You ungrateful wretch!" shouted the Beast in a dreadful voice. "I saved your life and, in return, you steal my roses! You shall die for it!"

The merchant fell to his knees and lifted up his hands. "My Lord," said he, "forgive me. I only wanted a rose for one of my daughters."

"My name is not Lord," replied the monster, "but Beast. Kind words will do you no good. But I will release you if one of your daughters will come willingly and take your place. You may go on your way if you swear that you or your daughter will return within three months."

The merchant was not going to give any of his daughters to the ugly monster, but he thought at least he could see them once more. So he promised he would return, and the Beast told him he could leave. The merchant took his horse out of the stable and left the palace with as much grief as he had entered it with joy.

In a few hours the merchant was home. "Here, Beauty," he said. "Take these roses. Little do you know how much they will cost your father." So saying, he told them all his adventures.

The two oldest sisters began to cry bitterly, but Beauty did not. "My Father," she said, "you shall not suffer on my account. I will take your place."

"No, Beauty," said the merchant. "I cannot let you."

"Indeed, Father," said Beauty, "you shall not go without me."

At the end of three months, Beauty and her father set
out. The horse took the direct road to the palace, and
towards evening, they saw it lit up as before. The horse
went by itself into the stable, and the good man and his
daughter entered the great hall. There they found a table
splendidly set, with two places laid.

The merchant did not feel like eating, but Beauty, trying
to appear cheerful, sat down. She thought, "The Beast
must want to fatten me up before he devours me."

After they had finished, they heard a terrible roar. Beauty trembled at the sight of the monster, but she did not turn away. The monster asked her if she came willingly, and she replied, "Yes."

"You are very good," said Beast. "Honest man, go on your way tomorrow morning and do not come here again. Good night, Beauty."

"Good night, Beast," she replied, and the monster left.

"Oh, daughter," said the merchant, "let me stay here."

"No, Father," said Beauty. "I shall stay."

After they had gone to bed, Beauty dreamed a fine lady came to her and said, "Beauty, I am content with your goodness. Your offer to give up your own life to save your father's will not go unrewarded."

On awakening, Beauty told her father the dream. But though it comforted him a little, he could not keep from crying as he bade his daughter farewell.

As soon as he had gone, Beauty sat down and began to cry, too. But then she thought, "It is silly to waste what little time I have left crying. I might as well explore the Beast's fine castle."

After walking around a little, Beauty was surprised to discover a door with BEAUTY'S ROOM written over it. She opened the door and found a richly furnished room, filled with books.

"Well," she said to herself, "if I were to live here only one day, Beast would not have taken such care for my comfort." She picked up a book and, opening it, read:

Welcome, Beauty, banish fear;
You are queen and mistress here.
Speak your wishes, speak your will,
Swift obedience meets them still.

"Alas," she said with a sigh. "All I want is to see my poor father."

No sooner had she spoken, than Beauty saw her own home in a large mirror on the wall. Her father had just arrived, looking very sorrowful. A moment later, everything vanished, including Beauty's fears.

That night as she sat down to supper, she heard Beast's terrible roar and could not help being frightened again.

"Beauty," said the monster when he appeared, "may I sit and watch while you eat? If my presence troubles you, I will leave. But tell me, do you think me very ugly?"

"Yes," said Beauty, "but I believe you are very good-natured."

"So I am," said the monster. "But besides being ugly, I am a silly, stupid creature."

"'Tis no sign of silliness to think so," replied Beauty, "for few who are slow-witted know it, and fewer still admit it."

"Eat then, Beauty," said the monster, "and amuse yourself in your palace, for everything here is yours."

Beauty had lost almost all her fear of the monster, when he said, "Beauty, will you be my wife?"

She did not answer at first, for she was afraid of making him angry. At last, however, she said, "No, Beast."

The poor monster gave such a great sigh, the whole palace shook. Then he said, "Good night, Beauty," and left the room.

For three months, Beast visited Beauty every night at nine. Each day, Beauty discovered some new quality in the monster, and seeing him so often, she grew used to his ugliness. Far from dreading his visit, she would often wait impatiently for the hour to come.

Only one thing bothered Beauty. Every night, before he bade her good night, the monster asked her if she would be his wife.

One evening she said to him, "Beast, I wish I could consent to marry you, but I cannot. I shall always value you as a friend. Try to be content with that."

"I will try to be content if you will promise never to leave me," said the Beast.

Beauty blushed, for in her mirror, she had seen that her father was ill from sorrow. "I could promise never to leave you," Beauty said, "but I want to see my father."

"I will send you to your father," said the monster, "and poor Beast will die of grief."

"I care for you too much," said Beauty. "I promise you to return in a week."

"You shall be there tomorrow morning," said the Beast. "When you are ready to come back, lay your ring on your night table before you go to sleep. Farewell, Beauty."

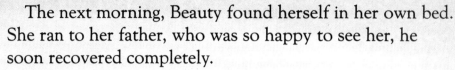

The next morning, Beauty found herself in her own bed. She ran to her father, who was so happy to see her, he soon recovered completely.

When Beauty told her sisters how happy she was with Beast, they could hardly contain their jealousy.

That night one sister said to the other, "Let us try to keep her here over a week. Perhaps the monster will be so angry at her for breaking her word, he will devour her."

After that, the sisters behaved kindly to Beauty. When the week had ended, they cried and carried on so much that Beauty agreed to stay for another week.

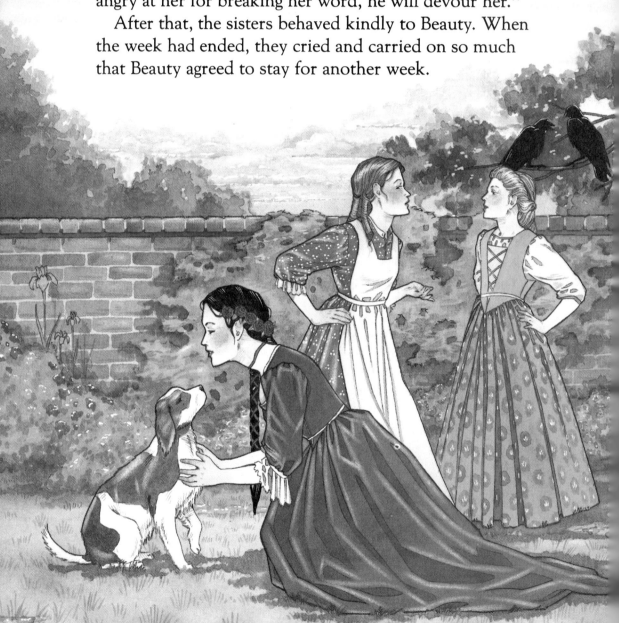

However, Beauty could not help thinking about Beast and the worry she must be causing him. The tenth night, she dreamed she saw Beast lying half-dead on the grass in the palace garden. Beauty woke up in tears.

"How can I be so unkind to Beast? Can he help it if he is ugly and has little sense? He is kind and good, and that is enough. It is true I am not in love with him, but I do care for him as a dear friend." Then Beauty put her ring on the table and went to sleep.

When she awoke, she was overjoyed to find herself in the Beast's palace. She put on one of her richest dresses to please him and waited impatiently for evening. At last the clock struck nine, but no Beast appeared.

Remembering her dream, Beauty ran out into the garden. There she found poor Beast stretched out in the grass. She fetched some water and washed his face.

Beast opened his eyes and said to Beauty, "You forgot your promise. I was so sad at losing you. But since I have the happiness of seeing you once more, I die satisfied."

"No, dear Beast," said Beauty, "you must not die! Live to be my husband! Alas! I thought I only cared for you as a friend, but now I see I cannot live without you."

All at once the palace blazed with lights, fireworks went off, and music began to play. Beauty looked up in amazement. When she turned back, Beast had disappeared. In his place was a handsome Prince.

"Where is my dear Beast?" Beauty cried.

"You see him before you," said the Prince. "A wicked fairy turned me into a Beast and made me appear silly and stupid. In that shape and form I had to remain until a beautiful maiden consented to marry me. Though there are many who are beautiful, only you in the whole world could be won by the goodness of my heart."

Beauty and the Prince went together into the castle. There Beauty found the lady she had seen in her dream the first night.

"Beauty," said she, "you have chosen virtue over wit and beauty, and deserve to find someone in whom all three qualities are united."

The good fairy gave a stroke of her wand, and they were transported to the Prince's kingdom. His subjects received him with joy, and he and Beauty were married within the week. They lived together for years, and their happiness was complete.

The Frog Prince

ONE FINE evening a young Princess was out walking in the royal gardens. She carried a golden ball, which was her favorite plaything. As she walked, she tossed it into the air and caught it again as it fell. Each time she threw the ball up a little higher. At last she threw it so high, that when she stretched out her hand to catch it, she missed. The ball fell to the ground and rolled right into a nearby spring of water.

"Oh, no!" cried the Princess. She looked around for help, but there was no one in sight. She looked into the spring, but it was so deep, she couldn't see the bottom. "What will I ever do without my golden ball?" she said. "I'd give anything to get it back again."

At these words, a frog popped its head out of the water, startling the Princess.

"If you will let me live with you and eat from your plate and sleep on your bed," said the frog, "I will bring your ball back to you."

"I never heard a frog speak before," she thought. "But if he can speak, perhaps he can get my ball for me." She said, "If you will bring me my ball, I will do as you wish."

The frog put his head down and dived deep beneath the water. After a little while, he came back up with the golden ball in his mouth. He threw it on the ground, and the Princess picked it up and ran away as fast as she could.

The frog called after her, "Wait for me, Princess, and take me with you as you promised." But the Princess did not stop.

The next day, just as the Princess had sat down to dinner, she heard a *tap-tap-tap* on the door.

"Open the door, my Princess dear,
Open the door to your true love here!
Remember the words that you and I spoke
By the well spring under the oak."

The Princess ran to the door and opened it. There sat the frog. Before he could move, she shut the door and went back to her seat.

"Who was that?" asked her father, the King.

"A frog," she said. "He lifted my golden ball out of the spring for me last evening after I promised him he could come and live with me."

"You made a promise," said the King. "Now you must keep it. Go and let him in."

The Princess did as she was told, and the frog hopped into the room and up onto the table next to her plate. After they shared her dinner, the frog said, "I am tired. Carry me upstairs to your bed."

The Princess picked him up and carried him upstairs. The frog hopped to her pillow, where he slept all night long. In the morning, he jumped off the bed, hopped downstairs, and went out of the castle.

But no sooner had the Princess sat down to dinner that night than she heard the familiar *tap-tap-tap* at the door. When she opened it, the frog came in and shared her dinner and slept on her pillow until morning.

The third night he did the same, but in the morning the Princess awoke to find a handsome Prince watching her from the foot of the bed.

"Who are you?" she asked in astonishment. "How did you get in here?"

"I am he whom you knew as a frog," said the Prince. "A wicked fairy enchanted me. You have broken her spell by letting me share your dinner and sleep on your bed for three nights. Will you marry me and come with me to my father's kingdom?"

"I will," said the young Princess without hesitation.

So they were married and lived happily for many years.

The Six Swans

ONE DAY, while hunting in a great wood, a King chased a wild boar so quickly that no one could keep up with him. When evening came, he found that he had lost his way. Then he saw a very old woman coming towards him through the trees. She was a witch, but the King did not know it.

"My good woman," said he, "can you show me the way out of the wood?"

"Yes, my Lord King," she answered, "on one condition. I have a daughter who is as fair as any in the world. If you will make her your Queen, I will show you the way. Otherwise you will die here."

As the King did not want to die in the wood, he agreed. The old woman led him to her little house.

Though the daughter was very beautiful, the King could not look at her without an inward shudder. Nevertheless, he took her before him on his horse, and the old woman showed him the way. Soon he was home again, and the wedding was held a few days later.

Now the King had been married before, and his first
wife had left seven children, six boys and one girl, whom
he loved dearly. Fearing the stepmother might treat them
badly, he took them to a castle in the middle of a forest
where they were well-hidden. Even the King could not
find the castle without a ball of yarn a wise woman had
given him. When he threw it down before him, it unrolled
itself and showed him the way.

The King was away from home so often, that at last the
Queen grew angry. She bribed his servants with gold, and
they told her the King's secret.

After that, the Queen did not rest until she had found out where the King kept the yarn. Then she made some little white silk shirts and sewed a charm into each. One day when the King had gone hunting, she took the shirts and the ball of yarn and went to the castle.

The children thought it was their father coming, and the brothers ran joyfully to meet him. When they came near, the wicked Queen threw a little shirt over each one. As soon as the shirts touched their bodies, they were changed into swans, and flew away. The Queen did not know about the daughter, who had waited in the castle.

The next day the King went to see his children and found only his daughter.

"Where are your brothers?" he asked her.

She told him what she had seen from her window. Never dreaming it was the Queen who had enchanted his sons, the fearful King wished to take his daughter home. But she would not go.

"I must seek my brothers," she said to herself. That evening she ran away and went straight into the forest.

She walked all that night and the next day, until she could walk no longer. At last she came to a clearing near a stream, and lay down under some bushes to rest.

Near sunset, she heard a rustling sound and saw six swans alight in the clearing. They blew at one another until they had blown off all their feathers. Then each stripped off his swanskin as if it had been a shirt.

When the maiden saw her brothers, she came out from under the bushes. The brothers were as happy to see their sister as she was to see them, but their joy did not last long.

"We can only take our human shape every evening for a quarter of an hour," the brothers said. "After that we are changed again into swans."

"Can I do nothing to set you free?" the maiden asked.

"Oh, no," they answered. "It would be too hard. For six whole years you could never speak or laugh. And during that time you would have to make six shirts out of nettles. If you were to say a single word before the six years were ended, all your work would be for nothing."

At that the quarter of an hour came to an end, and the brothers changed into swans and flew away.

The maiden made up her mind to set her brothers free. She went into the middle of the forest, where she climbed a tree and went to sleep.

The next morning she gathered nettles and began sewing. As for speaking, there was no one to speak to, and as for laughing, she had no mind to. After a long time, it happened that the King of that country went hunting, and saw the maiden in the tree.

"Who are you?" he called. "Come down. I will not harm you." When the maiden would not answer, two of the King's huntsmen climbed the tree and carried her down.

Moved by her beauty, the King took her to his castle. He spoke to her in every language he knew, but the maiden remained silent. Still, her gentle ways so pleased him that he said, "This maiden will I marry, and no other."

So the king and the maiden were wed. But the King's wicked stepmother did not think the unknown maiden was worthy of the King.

After a year passed, the Queen's first child was born. The old woman carried it away and hid it. Then she went to the King and told him his wife had eaten the child. The King would not believe such a thing, and ordered that no one should harm the Queen.

The next time a child was born, the wicked stepmother did the same thing. The King would still not believe her words. But when the old woman stole the third newborn child, the King could do nothing but give the Queen up to justice. The court sentenced her to death by fire.

The day on which the Queen was to die was the very last one of the sixth year during which she could neither speak nor laugh. Five of the shirts which were to free her brothers from the evil spell were ready, but the sixth still needed the left sleeve.

As the Queen was led to the great pile of wood, she carried the five finished shirts on her arm. She was still sewing the sixth as she mounted the pile.

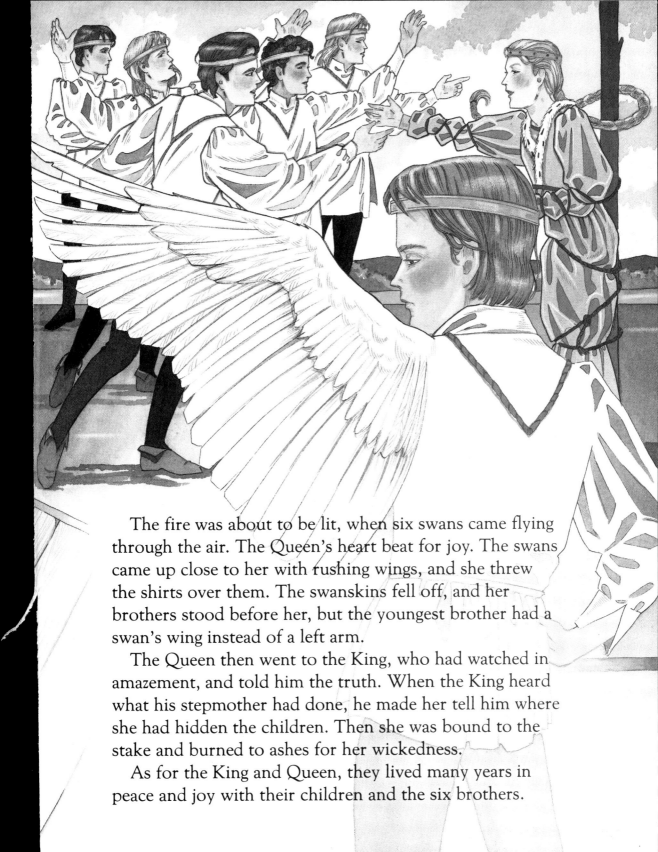

The fire was about to be lit, when six swans came flying
through the air. The Queen's heart beat for joy. The swans
came up close to her with rushing wings, and she threw
the shirts over them. The swanskins fell off, and her
brothers stood before her, but the youngest brother had a
swan's wing instead of a left arm.

The Queen then went to the King, who had watched in
amazement, and told him the truth. When the King heard
what his stepmother had done, he made her tell him where
she had hidden the children. Then she was bound to the
stake and burned to ashes for her wickedness.

As for the King and Queen, they lived many years in
peace and joy with their children and the six brothers.